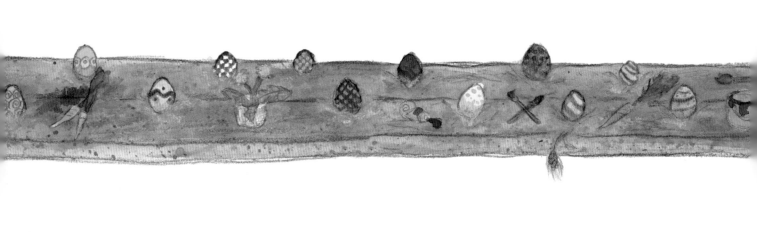

Copyright © 2005 by NordSüd Verlag AG, Gossau Zürich, Switzerland
First published in Switzerland under the title *Bravo, kleines Huhn!*
English translation copyright © 2006 by North-South Books Inc., New York

First published in the United States, Great Britain, Canada, Australia, and New Zealand
in 2006 by North-South Books, an imprint of NordSüd Verlag AG, Gossau Zürich, Switzerland.
Distributed in the United States by North-South Books Inc., New York.

Library of Congress Cataloging-in-Publication Data is available.
A CIP catalogue record for this book is available from The British Library.
ISBN 0-7358-2001-5 (trade edition) 10 9 8 7 6 5 4 3 2 1
ISBN 0-7358-2002-3 (library edition) 10 9 8 7 6 5 4 3 2 1
Printed in Belgium

ONE
MORE
EGG

Sarah Emmanuelle Burg

North-South Books / New York / London

One sunny spring day Bunny came hopping up to a young chicken.

"Please, dear Chicken, I need just one more egg. Will you lay it for me?"

"Me?" cried the chicken. "I can't lay eggs! I'm still too young. But if you really need that egg, Bunny, we could ask . . .

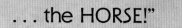
. . . the HORSE!"

"Hello, Horse," said the chicken.
"Would you please lay an egg for us?"

"Me? I don't lay eggs! I pull the cart and carry the crops to market," whinnied the horse.

"Come on, Bunny," said the chicken. "We'll ask . . .

. . . the PIG!"

"Dear Pig, would you please lay
an egg for us?"

"Me? I don't lay eggs! My job is to take care of my little piglets," grunted the pig.

"Don't worry, Bunny," said the chicken. "We'll ask . . .

. . . the SHEEP!"

"Dear Sheep," said the chicken, giving her a big hug, "would you please lay an egg for us?"

"Me? I don't lay eggs. All I can give is my soft, warm wool," bleated the sheep.

"Well then, Bunny," said the chicken, "we'll ask . . .

. . . the COW!"

"Good day, dear Cow," said the chicken. "Would you please lay an egg for us?"

"Me? I don't lay eggs! I make milk for the farmer," mooed the cow.

"Oh, well, Bunny," said the chicken, "let's ask . . .

. . . the MOLE!"

"Hello, Mole," said the chicken. "Could you please lay an egg for us?"

"Me? I don't lay eggs! I dig long tunnels underground," chirped the mole. "But why don't you ask him, . . .

"Come on!" cried the bunny, terrified.

And they ran as fast as they could to . . .

... the HENS!

"Dear Hens," begged the chicken,
"Bunny needs just one more egg.
Could one of you please lay it?"

"We?" cackled the hens. "We already gave him our eggs. You're old enough to lay one yourself. All you have to do is press really hard."

So the chicken pressed really hard!

She pressed

and pressed

and pressed

and . . .

out popped an egg!

"Look, Bunny!" the chicken called proudly, "I have the egg for you! I laid it myself— my very first egg! But tell me, what did you need it for anyway?"

"*That*, dear Chicken," said the bunny with a mischievous wink, "*that* is a secret."

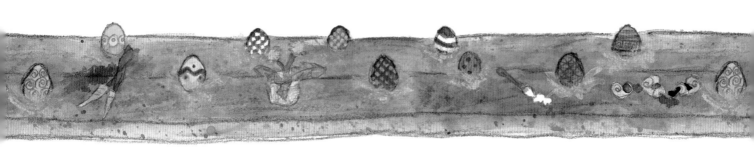